The Courage of the
Little Hummingbird

A Tale Told Around the World

By Leah Henderson Illustrated by Magaly Morales

Abrams Books for Young Readers

New York

Across oceans, lands, and skies. In villages, in towns, in cities, and classrooms. In whispers, in shouts, and in many different languages, the story of the little hummingbird of the Great Forest is told.

Long, long ago . . .

Flames crackled and leaped. Tree branches snapped. Leaves crinkled. The Great Forest was ablaze.

Animals dashed in every direction. They had no choice but to scurry away from the place they all called home.

The fire sprang higher and higher
as a troop of baboons,
a shadow of jaguars,

a roll of armadillos,

a nest of snakes,

a bed of sloths,

a litter of rabbits,

and a pandemonium of parrots
all fled—scared and unsure.

The little hummingbird hovered for a moment, wary, as the long trail of animals waded into the river or flew across its waters.

On the safer shore, the lion shook ash from his mane.

The chimpanzee swung from a tree and pointed back at the flames.

The elephant stamped her feet.

And the bear licked
his wounded paw.

None of them nor the other animals dared
move back toward the fire.

But the little hummingbird thought of each branch and each tree that
protected so many of the animals, and the nectar of each flower that
fed her. How could she leave them helpless in the raging flames?

She swooped down, flitted her wings, and asked, "Are we going to let it all burn?"

"The fire's too mighty," growled the lion.

"But you're the mightiest beast there is! Isn't there something you can do?"

"The flames are much too high," cried the giraffe.

"Even for you? Your head reaches the clouds!"

"Can't you see the fire is too angry?" bellowed the elephant.

"What if you calm it with sprays of water from your trunk?" questioned the little hummingbird. "There must be something we can do."

"Nonsense," croaked the frog.

"It's too late," said the woodland penguin.

"It's hopeless," muttered the fox.

"Unfortunately," the wise old turtle declared, "there's nothing to be done."

The little hummingbird disagreed. She couldn't bear to see their forest home burn. But what could she do to help?

The other animals stayed gathered, making sure everyone had made it out safe. Suddenly, the little hummingbird became a streak of color racing across the sky. She dove deep, skimmed the river, and filled her tiny beak with water. Then she darted toward the flames.

"Wait!" cried the mongoose. But the little hummingbird zipped straight for the roaring fire.

"No!" howled the hyena.

"Stop!" bleated the okapi.

"What's she doing?" squealed the aardvark.

"Oh, that senseless hummingbird!" screeched the owl. "She thinks she can make a difference."

Ignoring the shouts of her friends, the little hummingbird
neared the heat and flames. Smoke hissed around her.
Ash weighed down her wings.

She opened her beak and released
a single drop of water.

The fire continued to rage.

The little hummingbird returned to the water's edge. She scooped up another beakful of liquid, and then raced back through the blanket of gray.

Over and over, she rushed from flame to water, water to flame.

The animals watched in disbelief.

Smoke stung her eyes, and a ribbon of coughs tumbled across the sky when her beak was empty.

Even when her delicate wings got singed, she didn't give up. She flew back and forth.

One drop.

Then another.

Then one drop more.

Finally, the lion roared, "Enough of this! You're too small.
A few specks of water won't settle this fury!
What do you think you're doing?"

The other animals agreed.

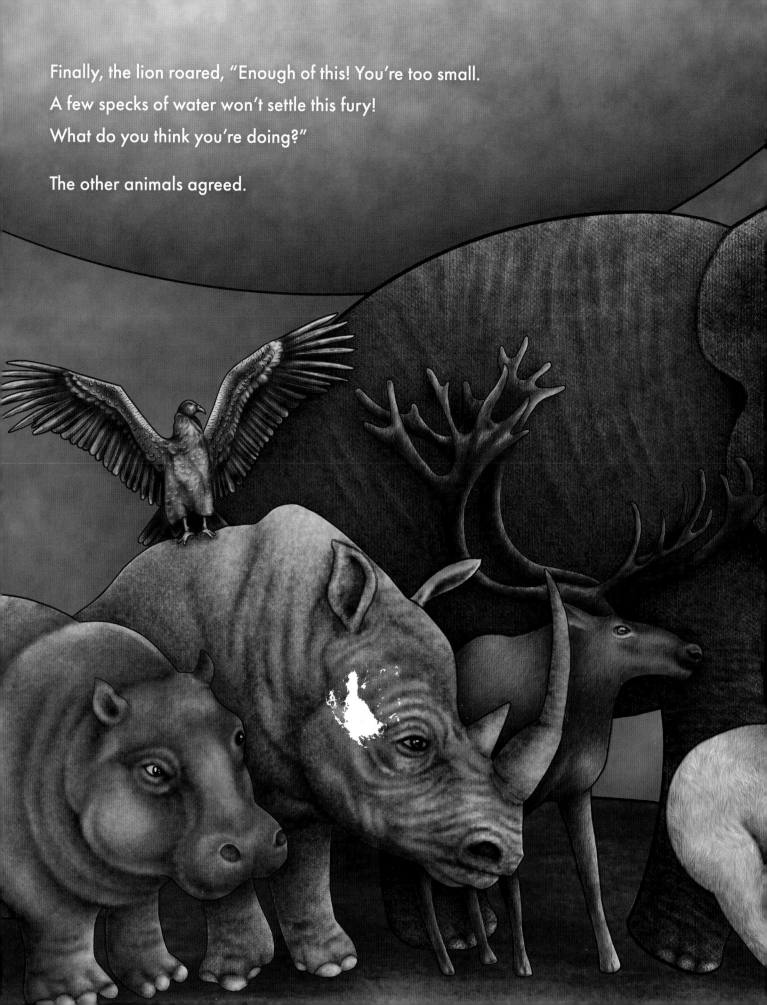

Before taking another drop of water into her beak,
the little hummingbird turned to the lion, the rhino, the
elephant, and all the animals of the Great Forest that
were bigger and stronger than her and said,

"I'm doing all I can."

A quiet hush spread across the jumble of animals.

Then the lion looked at the chimpanzee, and the chimpanzee looked at the okapi. The okapi turned to the giraffe, and the giraffe turned toward the bear. But it was the elephant that stepped forward first, breaking the surface of the river with her trunk. Soon all the animals, both large and small, gathered side by side along the water's edge.

Ready to do all they could to save their forest home.

Together.

Author's Note

In this retelling of the story of the little hummingbird and in many other versions that I have heard, the great forest or jungle is home to animals from every corner of the globe. Elephants share space with armadillos, and tigers roam alongside bears and lions, as do other animals that are generally not found in the same ecosystems. Other times, storytellers include only animals familiar to where they live. The origins of this fable are believed to have started with the Quechua people of modern-day Ecuador in South America. Through many translations and retellings, the story has stretched and grown, as stories often do, but the heart and courage of the little hummingbird has never wavered and has always stayed true. The tale conveys the importance of doing all we can even when we confront overwhelming odds.

I first heard this fable when I was young, and I like to think it was shared during a moment when I felt a challenge was too great or that my efforts would not be enough. No matter when or where the story was first told to me, I am not alone in being inspired by the courage of the little hummingbird.

The late Kenyan activist and Nobel Prize winner Wangari Maathai spoke of first hearing the tale on a trip to Japan, and often said, "I will be a hummingbird; I will do the best I can." Inspired in part by the story, she began a conservation movement across her homeland. She started by planting a few trees, and—through the help of the Green Belt Movement, an organization she founded in 1977—she encouraged others to "Be a hummingbird!" This led to more than 51 million trees being planted throughout Kenya. French writer and environmentalist Pierre Rabhi believed the story of the hummingbird was an excellent example for people who asked, "What can I do?" And when children's rights activist Kailash Satyarthi, who has set out to end child labor all over the world, gave his Nobel Prize acceptance speech, he even referenced a story he remembered from his childhood in India about the courageous little hummingbird. Through the hummingbird's example, he encourages others to do their bit "to help ensure every child is free to be a child." Each of these global citizens reminds us that with one tree, one step, one breath—or in my case, one word after the next—we can all be like that little hummingbird and begin to make a lasting impact and change.

So why not be the little hummingbird and do all you can?

Artist's Note

The story of this hummingbird provides a lesson from which we can all learn. The hummingbird plays a role in many cultures. In my country of Mexico, there are stories about the tiny bird. A legend of the Mayan culture tells that the ancient gods created all the things and animals of this world. One day they took a jade stone and they shaped it into a very small arrow that when they blew on it became a hummingbird. Hummingbirds shine like the sun and reflect all the colors of the world. The Mayans believed the mission of the birds was to carry from here to there the thoughts of women, men, and even the gods themselves. So, if someone wishes you well, a hummingbird will take this desire and bring it to you, or it will take your best thoughts to others.

The Aztec or Mexicas, Mesoamerican people, considered hummingbirds to be brave fighters. The birds were a symbol of Huitzilopochtli, the god of war.

The Courage of the Little Hummingbird and these ancient stories tell us about strength, bravery, and courage, but also of love, empathy, and sharing our best thoughts with those around us. Likewise, they explain how these thoughts help us to understand that we are part of a whole and to recognize the bonds that keep us together. Scholars say that understanding this gives fullness and meaning to life, but also helps us recognize that being part of a whole can change our world in a positive way.

Says a very wise axiom: "Everything is more than the sum of its parts."

Where Do These Animals Live?

In this version of *The Little Hummingbird*, the Great Forest is home to animals from every corner of the globe. Here is where some of these animals are typically found:

aardvarks: Africa

anteaters: Central and South America

armadillos: South, Central, and North America

baboons: Africa and Arabia

badgers: North America

chimpanzees: Africa

deer: All continents except Antarctica and Australia

elephants: Africa and Southeast Asia

giraffes: Africa

gorillas: Central Africa

grasshoppers: All continents except Antarctica

iguanas: Central and South America, Caribbean Islands

impalas: Africa

hippopotamuses: Africa

hummingbirds: North and South America

hyenas: Africa, Arabia, and Asia

jaguars: North, South, and Central America

lemurs: Madagascar (Africa)

lions: Africa and India

mongeese: Africa, Southern Asia, Iberia, Hawaii, Caribbean Islands

okapis: Africa

parrots: Africa, South, and Central America; Australia; Southeast and South Asia; Oceania

peacocks: Southeast Asia and Africa

pelicans: All continents except Antarctica

penguins, woodland (snares): New Zealand

raccoons: North, Central, and South America; Caribbean Islands

red foxes: North America

rhinoceroses: Africa, South and Southeast Asia

sloths: South and Central America

snails: Mediterranean, Western Europe, and Northern Africa

squirrels: The Americas, Eurasia, and Africa

toucans: Southern Mexico, Central and South America

turtles: North America and South Asia

wolves: North America, Europe, Asia, and North Africa

Did You Know?

The hummingbird in this story undertakes a tremendous task, despite her size. A tiny hummingbird is amazing in many ways. Here are a few:

- The Americas are the only natural habitat of the hummingbird. They can be found as far south as Chile and as far north as Alaska.

- There are 365 species or different kinds of hummingbirds. The size of a hummingbird egg is between a coffee bean and a jellybean.

- The smallest species of hummingbird is also the smallest bird in the world and can weigh less than a penny.

- Hummingbirds are the only birds that fly backward, up and down, sideways, and even upside down.

- Hummingbirds beat their wings an average of 50–80 beats per second, making them appear as a blur to the human eye. The fast movement also creates a humming sound—and that's where they got their name.

- Hummingbirds have little to no sense of smell, but they see farther than a human and hear better than one, too.

- Hummingbirds have a third eyelid, like a set of flight goggles, that protect their eyes as they zip around.

- Hummingbirds have great memories—they remember every flower and every feeder they visit.

- Hummingbirds visit an average of 1,000 flowers each day for nectar.

- Hummingbirds may eat every 10–15 minutes and have up to 48 small meals in a day!

- A group of hummingbirds can be a glittering, a shimmer, a tune, a bouquet, a hover, or a charm.

To all the world's little hummingbirds—thank you!
—L.H.

A Rodrigo y Quetzally, mi pequeño gran esfuerzo por cambiar el mundo.
To Rodrigo and Quetzally, my little great effort to change the world.
—M.M.

The illustrations for this book were made with digital media.

Cataloging-in-Publication Data has been applied for and
may be obtained from the Library of Congress.

ISBN 978-1-4197-5455-5

Text © 2023 Leah Henderson
Illustrations © 2023 Magaly Morales
Edited by Howard W. Reeves
Book design by Heather Kelly

Printed and bound in China
10 9 8 7 6 5 4 3 2 1

Abrams Books for Young Readers are available at special discounts when purchased
in quantity for premiums and promotions as well as fundraising or educational use.
Special editions can also be created to specification. For details,
contact specialsales@abramsbooks.com or the address below.

Abrams® is a registered trademark of Harry N. Abrams, Inc.

ABRAMS The Art of Books
195 Broadway, New York, NY 10007
abramsbooks.com